MW01065022

The CODE RED CASES

by Alice Alfonsi

Illustrated by Rich Harrington

Table of Contents

Mystery #1

Mystery #2

Mystery #3

Itching to crack a M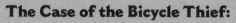stery?

Well, get ready! In this book, you'll find three puzzling cases:

 The Case of the Bicycle Thief:
At the end of a birthday party, a girl realizes that her prized present is missing. Who stole it?

 The Case of the Innocent Art Student:
Someone spray paints illegal graffiti on a school's front wall. The principal accuses the wrong person. Can you figure out who really did it and why?

 The Case of the Suspicious Spelling Bee:
A girl who was never a very good speller wins a major spelling bee. Did she cheat? And if she did, who helped her?

The best thing about these mysteries is that you get to solve them yourself! That's right. Find out what it's like to be a case cracking detective and see if you can figure out the answer to these mysteries. Here's how:

- **Look for clues:** In each case, you'll find clues that point to suspects and their motives. Read carefully, or you'll miss them!

- **Study the crime scene:** Your kit includes photos of each crime scene and major evidence for you to examine.

- **Use the red decoder:** Each *U-Solve-It! Mysteries* book comes with a set of tools that you can use to solve the crime. In this pack, you'll find hidden clues and a special red decoder. Use them together to reveal info that will help you solve each case.

When you've cracked each *Code Red* case, head to the *U-Solve-It!* web site at **www.scholastic.com/usolveit**. You'll need this password:

REDALERT

Mystery #1

Mystery #2

Mystery #3

The Case of the Bicycle Thief

1. THE MISSING PRESENT

"Rob?" called my little sister, Laurel, from the family room.

"What?" I shouted.

On a typical Saturday, I was hangin' at the skatepark, catching air with my friends. But on this particular Saturday, I wasn't. My mom had roped me into helping her throw a birthday party for my little sister.

Yeah, you heard right. My skateboarding buds were laughing themselves silly when I told them, but the truth is... I didn't mind. Laurel's a pretty good sister, for a girl. She hardly ever cries. She's not a bad "Player 2" on my video games. Plus, she'll clean my room for seventy-five cents and an ice cream cone.

Anyway, I'm almost fourteen now, and when I turned nine, I didn't have a birthday party. So I wanted Laurel to have one. And I wanted it to be really cool and fun. As it

7

turned out, Laurel's party *was* really cool and fun. But not what happened after it.

"Where's my new bike?" Laurel shouted.

I was in the kitchen, bagging up the overflowing garbage can. The kids from Laurel's birthday party had left about twenty minutes ago. We waved goodbye to the last one, and then started cleaning up.

Laurel's friends were fun, but they were total pigs. They left behind a mountain of paper plates, cups, napkins, and plastic silverware covered with cake crumbs and melted ice cream.

I finished bagging the garbage and plopped it in the can outside the back door. Then I washed my hands at the sink and walked into the family room.

"What are you shouting about, Laurel?" I asked. "Your

new bike's right there—"

I stopped and stared. A card table stacked with Laurel's presents sat near the back wall of the family room. But her biggest and best present of all was no longer there. Laurel's new bike was gone.

"I left it right here, Rob," Laurel said. She was pointing with one hand, scratching her head of damp brown curls with the other. "It was leaning against the wall, right next to the card table. Right here, under your sign."

I'd made a big *Happy Birthday, Laurel* sign with my mom's computer printer. I'd printed out one huge letter at a time. Then I'd hung them up to spell the birthday message.

"I didn't move your new bike," I told my sister.

"Do you think Mom moved it?" Laurel asked.

"If she did, we can't ask her," I replied. "She just left for work."

Our mom worked as a nurse at the Montgomery County Hospital Emergency Room. She usually worked the day shift on Saturday. Because of Laurel's party, she switched with another ER nurse who worked from four to midnight.

Laurel and I used to have a dad, too. He was a police officer. Sergeant Robert Jerome Hollinger was his name. (That's my name too, except for the sergeant part.) Anyway, he died four years ago, the week of my birthday. That's why I didn't have a party when I turned nine. I guess that's also why

I felt sort of protective of my little sister. She didn't have a dad anymore, but she had me.

"Mom must have moved my bike!" Laurel insisted.

I shook my head. "Why would she do that? And where would she move it?"

Laurel frowned. "Will you help me look around the house?"

2. THE SEARCH

We looked in every room. We looked in the basement and all the closets. Then we looked in the back yard. Our yard was fenced in. It wasn't really big, but it had one great feature—a built-in pool.

Our family didn't have a lot of money, but the pool was something that my dad had decided to splurge on. In high school, his swim team had won the state championship. He was a really strong swimmer. I still remembered how he used to do laps every morning before going to work.

Anyway, that's why Laurel's party had been a pool party too. We already had this great pool. And it was early June. The weather was warm and sunny in the afternoons with clear, blue skies.

The party had run pretty smoothly. After the kids played a few games in our family room, Laurel opened her presents. Then the kids changed into their swimsuits, and they all played in the pool the rest of the afternoon.

That's another reason my mom wanted me around today. She knew I was a really strong swimmer, just like my dad. And she wanted me to help make sure the kids played safely in the water. (So here's me all afternoon: "Hey! No horsing around! No dunking! Yeah, I mean you!")

Funny, huh? Me as a swim cop. But it was actually pretty cool. My mom even gave me a whistle. Unfortunately, blowing the whistle now wasn't going to help my sister.

"Rob, where could it be?" Laurel cried after we couldn't find the bike out back.

"Let's keep looking," I said.

We checked around the east side of the house. Then we checked the front porch and yard. Finally, we checked the house's west side.

"What's this?" I murmured.

"What's what?" Laurel asked.

"This," I said and pointed into the bushes.

3. GETTING A CLUE

I moved toward the line of high bushes that grew along the west side of our house. Inside the dark green leaves of one bush, I saw a spot of bright pink color. I reached into the bush and pulled out a thin strip of material.

"It looks like a ribbon!" Laurel snatched it out of my hands.

"Have you seen it before?" I asked.

"Mom used pink ribbons like this to decorate the two presents she gave me," Laurel said.

Our mom gave Laurel her presents after breakfast this morning. The first present was a new pair of jeans. She'd wrapped that up in a gift box and decorated it with a pink ribbon.

The really big present Laurel got from our mom was the new bike. Laurel had wanted that bicycle for two years. It was a huge surprise. Laurel jumped around the house when she got it. Then she called her best friends to tell them.

Our mom hadn't wrapped the bike up. She'd just wheeled it into the family room with bright pink ribbons tied to the handlebars.

I looked at the pink ribbon in Laurel's hands. "Did you bring any of your presents out here today?" I asked. That would have explained the ribbon in the bushes.

Laurel shook her head. "No. I wore my new jeans to the party. And the bike never left the family room."

"Are you sure?" I asked.

"Sure, I'm sure!" Laurel said. "Remember? After you guys pushed back the furniture and rolled up the rug, I rode it around inside for fun. I was going to take it outside, but I couldn't. Mia and Kelly rang the doorbell, and Mom told me I had to start 'being a hostess' for my birthday party guests."

Mia and Kelly were twin sisters. They were the first two guests to arrive for Laurel's party. Their mom had dropped them off an hour early because she had to work at the mall.

I looked at the ribbon in Laurel's hand. Then I looked at the bushes again. Just to make sure the bike wasn't in those bushes, I squeezed between two of them. Now I was in our neighbors' yard.

Could our neighbors have taken the bike?

That seemed unlikely. Mr. and Mrs. Taglia were an older couple. They were both retired from their jobs, and they liked to travel in their RV. Last week, they left for a camping trip. Their house looked deserted, and the RV was still gone from their driveway.

"Come on," I said after I squeezed back between two of the high bushes. I turned the knob to the side door. It would have led us right back into the family room. But the door was locked.

"That's right," I said.

"What?" Laurel asked.

"Mom locked this door before we started cleaning up." I shrugged and we walked around to the rear of the house.

We went in the kitchen door and walked back into the family room, where we'd started our search. Balloons were still bobbing all over the room. The remains of the sunflower piñata still dangled from the ceiling.

Before the party, my mom and I had pushed the family room's sofa and armchairs against the walls. We'd also rolled up the area rug to make space for Laurel and her friends to play games. Everything looked the same as it had during the party—except the bike was gone.

I took the pink ribbon from Laurel and stuffed it into my jeans pocket. *This has to be a clue,* I told myself. *But a clue to what?*

4. A LIKELY SUSPECT

"So where's my bike, Rob?" Laurel asked. "Where is it?!"

My sister wasn't crying or anything. But she started pacing around the family room like a hamster in a cage. She threw up her hands, shook her head, and started pulling at her hair.

"Chill, Laurel," I said. "Don't freak."

"Don't tell me not to freak!" she cried. "You'd freak if you were me! That was my special present from Mom! What do you think she's going to say if I tell her the bike's lost?"

"It can't be lost," I said. "It's too big to be lost."

She stopped pacing and faced me. Her hands were on her hips. "Then what happened to my bike?" she demanded.

"I'm sorry, Laurel," I said. "But I think somebody took it."

"No." she said. "No way."

I knew this wouldn't be easy. People never want to believe something bad can happen to them. And when it does, the first thing they want to do is pretend that it didn't.

"Like I said, I'm sorry," I repeated as gently as I could. "But it's the only logical explanation. Somebody took your bike."

Laurel looked like a party balloon that suddenly lost all its air. She walked over to the sofa and sank down heavily into

its cushions. I sat down next to her.

"Somebody from the party took it," Laurel said. "That's what you think, isn't it?"

"It makes the most sense, doesn't it?" I

said. "I mean, think about it. If some random burglar did it, why didn't he or she take anything else?"

Laurel looked around. There was a laptop computer on the shelf in the corner. There was a TV set and a DVD player, still in the entertainment cabinet. And Laurel's other presents were still stacked on that card table beneath her *Happy Birthday* sign.

"But who?" Laurel asked. "I can't imagine any friend of mine doing this."

"Whoever did this isn't your friend," I said. "Which means…"

"What?" Laurel pressed.

"Did you have a fight with anyone at the party?" I asked.

"You know I didn't!" Laurel cried. "Everyone had a good time!"

"I didn't mean you fought at the party," I said. "I mean, did you have a fight lately with any of the kids who came to the party? Maybe one of your friends is holding a grudge."

Laurel didn't have to think long. "Willa," she said.

"Willa Churchill?" I asked. "She's one of your best friends."

"But she wouldn't come to the party today," Laurel said. "Didn't you notice?"

I shrugged. "You had, like, ten girls and six boys here. When I wasn't snapping Polaroid pictures for your 'Birthday

Scrapbook,' I was making sure nobody drowned in the pool, so I was a little busy."

"Yeah, well, Willa wasn't here, okay?" Laurel said.

"Why?" I asked. "Did you diss her or something?"

"No!" Laurel leaped to her feet. "I like Willa. It was really lame of her not to come."

"So why didn't she?" I asked.

Laurel sighed. "She wanted me to un-invite the twins—Mia and Kelly. And I wouldn't."

"Why doesn't she like Mia and Kelly?" I asked.

"Because…" Laurel shrugged. "She says they're dorks."

"That's mean. Why does she say that?" I asked.

"Because they're teacher's pets, and they both got to sing solos with the school choir at the Spring Festival two weeks ago."

I rolled my eyes. "I remember the Festival. Mom made me go to see you sing. I thought that show would never end."

Laurel pouted. "You said it was cool."

"Sorry," I said. "You were good, but it was boring. Today's party was cool though, except for this happening. You better tell me more about Willa and why she's mad at you."

Laurel nodded and began to pace. She explained that Willa really wanted to get one of the solos at the Festival. But Mia and Kelly had beaten her out. In Laurel's opinion, Willa's "tryout song" had sounded a lot better than Kelly's.

But the music teacher said it would look cuter on stage to have identical twins sing the solos, one right after the other.

"And that's why Willa can't stand them?" I asked. "Because they got to sing solos and she didn't?"

Laurel nodded. "She told me that if I didn't un-invite the dork twins, then she wasn't coming."

"But Mom is really good friends with their mother," I pointed out.

"I know," Laurel said. "I told Willa that, but she didn't care. I even called her this morning to tell her about my bike, but she was still angry. She said I'd chosen who I wanted to be friends with, so I couldn't be hers anymore. Then she hung up."

"Wait a second," I said.

"What?" Laurel asked.

I stood up from the couch. "Didn't you have a solo on Festival night, too?"

"Yeah, I did. I was the third soloist that night. After Mia and Kelly, I sang five lines alone. It wasn't as long as their solos, but…" Laurel shrugged.

"So you beat out Willa, just like Mia and Kelly?" I asked.

"I guess," Laurel said, "but…"

"But nothing," I said. "That's just one more reason for Willa to be angry with you."

"So you think she did it?" Laurel asked. "Willa Churchill took my bike to hurt me?"

I ticked off four facts on my fingers. "She knew you got a bike for a birthday present because you called her this morning to tell her. She knew the present was important to you. She was really angry at you. And she wasn't at the party."

"Why is that important?" Laurel asked. "That she wasn't at the party?"

"Because we saw everyone leave the house," I said. "None of your party guests took the bike with them or we would have noticed."

"You're right!" Laurel said. "Willa must have done it. She must have snuck into the house when we were all out back, swimming in the pool!"

"It's possible," I said.

"I'm going over to see Willa right now!" Laurel cried. "And you're coming with me!"

"I am?"

Laurel grabbed my hand and pulled. With a sigh, I followed my sister toward the front door. Then I stopped.

"Let's not risk any more thefts, okay?" I said.

I went back to chain the back door, check the locked side door, and bolt the front door right behind me.

5. GUILTY OR NOT GUILTY?

Willa Churchill lived at the end of our street. When we reached her lawn, Laurel started for her front path right away. I pulled her back.

"Wait here by the curb," I whispered. "I'm going to do a little snooping."

I snuck carefully around the grounds, looking for any sign of Willa's guilt. *Maybe I'll find another pink ribbon*, I thought. *Seeing the actual bike wouldn't hurt, either!*

But I didn't see anything suspicious—not in the back yard or at the sides of the house. Nothing in the front yard, either, or we would have seen it right away.

Willa's house was a ranch style. It was long and flat, and it didn't have a basement. But the big garage had windows at the top. I stood on tiptoes and peeked inside. There was a dark blue sedan parked in there. There was also a kid's tricycle, a pair of skis, and a weight bench. But Laurel's bike wasn't in there, either.

"No sign of your bike yet," I told Laurel. "Let's go talk to Willa now."

Laurel hit the doorbell. Mrs. Churchill answered.

"Oh, hi, Laurel!" she said brightly. "How are you? And Rob, isn't it?"

"Yes, Mrs. Churchill," I said. "Hi."

"Is Willa here?" Laurel asked.

"Sure, come on in." We walked into the living room. Willa's dad was reading the newspaper. Her little brother was watching cartoons on TV.

"Willa's in her bedroom. You know the way, Laurel," Mrs. Churchill told us before heading into the kitchen.

Laurel led me through the living room and down a hallway. She knocked on a closed door.

"Who is it?" Willa called.

"It's Laurel. Open the door!" my sister called.

"Laurel?!" Willa cried from inside her room. For a few seconds, we heard some suspicious shuffling. Then she opened the door.

Willa Churchill was a little taller than my sister. She had straight blond hair and glasses. And she looked really surprised to see us.

"What are you two doing here?" she asked.

"I need to talk to you," Laurel said.

"We both do," I said.

Willa pushed up her glasses and stared at me. "Why?"

"Can we just go in your room and talk?" Laurel asked.

Willa stomped back into her room. We followed.

Inside Willa's room, I saw a desk with a chair, a bed, a dresser, a bookshelf, and a closet with the door shut. *No bike,* I thought. Or, at least, there was none that I could *see*. She could have stashed it in another room of the house.

Willa sat on the bed, and I grabbed the desk chair. Laurel stood in the middle of the room with her arms crossed.

"What do you want to talk about?" Willa asked.

Laurel's brows knitted together. There was a long pause, and I realized my sister wasn't sure what to say. So I jumped in.

"We want to know where you were today," I asked.

"Why?" Willa shrugged. "I mean, you know where I *wasn't*. I wasn't at Laurel's party. She knows that." Then Willa frowned and looked at the floor. "Was it fun?" she asked in a little voice.

"Yes," I said.

"But it would have been more fun," Laurel added softly, "if you had come."

"Really?" Willa asked.

"Really," Laurel said.

"Well…I'm sorry I didn't," she admitted. "I should have. I mean, I was thinking about you all day. I even walked over to your house. I could hear the kids laughing in the back by the pool. But I felt sort of stupid about showing up after I told you that I wasn't going to."

"Is that when you took my bike?" Laurel asked.

Willa's jaw dropped. "What? What are you talking about?"

"She's talking about the bike she just got as a birthday gift. It vanished sometime during the party. Did you take it?" I asked.

Willa leaped off the bed. "No way! Why would I do something like that to my best friend?"

"Because you were angry," Laurel pointed out.

"I was angry. But I'm not anymore," Willa said. "I was going to make up with you. I just finished wrapping your present."

"You did?" Laurel asked.

Willa nodded. She went to her bookshelf and pulled down a basket. It was wrapped in bright red cellophane and tied with a pink ribbon.

"Here, Laurel," she said. "I was going to give this to you tomorrow. And say…you know, that I was sorry."

Laurel didn't open the gift, but she peeked inside. "Wow, this must have taken you a long time to put together."

Willa nodded. "I was shopping for weeks. There's like ten different nail polishes, hair clips, bubble baths—"

"Wow, this is really cool. Thanks, Willa."

Willa shrugged. "Happy Birthday, Laurel."

Laurel looked at me. "What do we do now, Rob?"

"That depends," I said.

"On what?" Laurel asked.

"On whether you believe Willa didn't take your bike," I said.

Willa folded her arms. "I'm telling the truth."

Laurel chewed her lip a moment, thinking it over. "I believe her," she finally said. "But if she didn't take it, then who did?"

"I bet I can tell you who did," Willa said. "Jilly Peterson."

"Jilly Peterson? No way," Laurel said. "She's always super nice."

Willa shook her head. "She's nice to everyone's face. But

do you know about her older sister?"

"Pam Peterson?" I asked. Pam was a grade ahead of me in middle school. She was the president of the Computer Club. She was really popular, too. She'd raised a lot of money for the club this year through online auctioning.

"Pam Peterson has a web page called Slam Girl," Willa told Laurel. "She slams kids she doesn't like."

"So," said Laurel. "That's Jilly's sister. Not Jilly."

"Wrong," Willa replied. "I just found out that Jilly's been using her sister's web page to totally diss people at our school. It's really mean. She calls herself Slam Girl Junior. And she slammed you and me both, Laurel."

6. PICTURE THIS

"I'm calling Jilly Peterson right now," Laurel said the moment we got home.

While my sister dialed, I tried to think about the details of the party. I still wasn't convinced that Willa was innocent. She could have named Jilly just to get the heat off herself.

If Jilly stole the bike, then when did she do it? I asked myself. *The bike was in the family room at the start of the party. And I didn't see any of the girls leave the party pedaling Laurel's bike! So the only time Jilly Peterson could have taken the bike was during the party, when we were all out back by the pool.*

That still seemed unlikely to me.

Nevertheless, I tried to remember who had gone inside the house alone after we started swimming. There had been only two kids. One was a girl. And one was a boy. Each said they had to use the bathroom. Each had gone into the house alone and come out alone.

I turned to ask Laurel a question. She was hanging up the phone.

"Jilly claims she didn't steal my bike," Laurel said. "But she knows who probably did."

"Who?" I asked.

"Jackson Maxwell." Laurel collapsed on the sofa like this was the worst news in the world. She dropped head on her lap and groaned.

"That news is actually pretty interesting," I said.

"Why?" Laurel asked, lifting her head.

"Because I remember there were only two people going into the house during the swimming part of the party. I just can't remember all your friends' names. But one was a girl with a yellow striped swim suit and one was a boy with electric blue jams."

"Where are the photos from the party?" Laurel asked.

I went to the table and picked up the small stack of photos sitting there.

"Mom took some of the party pictures to the hospital to show them off to her co-workers," I explained. "But she left enough here for us to look through."

Laurel leafed through the Polaroid photos. The ones at the top of the stack had been taken at the pool. In each of these photos, the kids were laughing and playing in the water.

The photos at the bottom of the stack had been taken indoors. Some showed Laurel opening her presents. And others showed the kids trying to hit the sunflower piñata.

The final photo in the stack looked funny.

"Weird. What's wrong with this photo?" Laurel asked. "It looks like it didn't develop right."

That's when I remembered. My mom had borrowed the Polaroid camera from me while I was busy being a "swim cop." She'd snapped two photos of my *Happy Birthday, Laurel* sign in the family room while all the kids were still playing in the pool. She joked to me that it was "hard evidence" for Laurel's scrapbook that I was actually a pretty good big brother.

I remembered her mentioning that one of the photos hadn't developed right. That's the one we were looking at now. My mom obviously took the other, good photo of my sign to work with her to show everyone.

"Forget that bad photo for now," I told Laurel. "Go back to the pool party photos. Which guy is Jackson Maxwell? Point him out."

Laurel pointed to a skinny boy in electric blue jams.

"That's him."

"Well," I said, "he's one of the two people who left the pool area saying he had to use the bathroom. Why does Jilly think he's the one who stole your bike?"

"Because she said he was caught stealing an iPod at school," Laurel said. "He took it from a girl's book bag in the cafeteria. But a teacher saw him do it. Jilly even told me the girl's name if I wanted to call her and check out the story."

"That's pretty bad, Laurel," I said. "If Jackson stole once, he might have done it again."

"But he's so nice to me!" Laurel wailed. "I know Jackson likes me."

"I'm sorry, but he looks pretty guilty," I said. "Unless…"

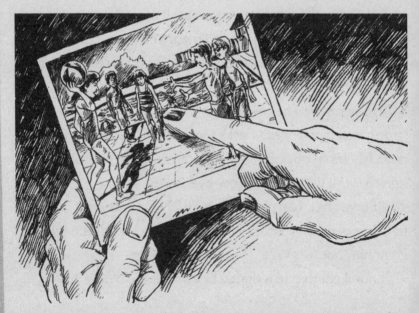

"What?" Laurel asked.

"Tell me who this girl is again?" I asked, pointing to the girl in a bright yellow striped swimsuit. "What's her name? Because she's the only other person I remember leaving the pool party to use the bathroom."

"Well, *that's* Jilly Peterson," Laurel said.

"Then she's still a suspect," I said.

"So what are you saying then, Rob? Do you think Jilly is lying? Do you think she could have done it?" Laurel asked.

"Jilly, Jackson, or..." I shrugged. "I'm sorry, but it still could have been Willa."

"How are we going to figure this out?" Laurel asked.

"I don't know..." I murmured.

I unrolled the family room's area rug and spread all the photos out on it. I kept looking at them, hoping to find some clue to help me catch the bicycle thief. I studied the details of each photo. But nothing jumped out at me. And I was beginning to feel like a failure.

I'll bet my dad could have solved this one, I told myself with a sigh.

"I just wish this one photo had come out better!" I cried in frustration.

"Which one?" Laurel asked.

I pointed to the only badly developed photo in the stack. The one my mom had taken.

"Why is that photo important?" Laurel asked.

"Because it's the only photo that was taken in the family room when we were all out by the pool," I said. "And the family room was the scene of the crime. Mom took the photo. She wanted a memento of my stupid *Happy Birthday, Laurel* sign."

"It's not a stupid sign, Rob. And I still say Willa is innocent." At the mention of Willa's name, Laurel suddenly remembered her birthday gift basket. "I mean, look what a cool present she put together for me. She must have gone to a dozen different stores...."

Laurel brought the basket over and sat down next to me on the rug. Then she untied the ribbon holding the red cellophane together. For a moment, the red film fell over the badly developed photo I'd been studying.

"Wait!" I cried as Laurel began to ball up the cellophane.

"What?" she asked.

"Give me that." I grabbed the red cellophane and smoothed it out. Then I placed it over the badly developed photo again.

Suddenly, I saw it. The filmy red paper fixed the messed up colors in the photo. Now I could see that the guilty party had left something behind on the family room floor—a clue.

This clue ruled out one of my suspects. But that still left two possible guilty parties. So I looked through the stack of party photos one more time.

I noticed a photo taken in the family room, during the beginning of the party. I studied the details of this photo. And then I smiled.

Wow, I thought, *I solved it.*

"I know who took your bike," I told my sister. "And I know how the thief did it. The clues are right here in these two photos."

Can you solve the Case of the Bicycle Thief?

Look at the two color photos from the party. Photo #1 developed normally. Photo #2 didn't—that's why some of its colors look funny. But if you use your red decoder, you'll be able to see the special hidden clue that helped Rob Hollinger solve this case. Was it Willa Churchill, Jilly Peterson, or Jackson Maxwell who took his sister's bike? Check out the U-Solve-It! *web site at* **www.scholastic.com/usolveit** *to see if you're right! You'll need this book's password to get in:*

REDALERT

The Case of the Innocent Art Student

TUESDAY, SEPTEMBER 25
3:15 P.M.
WEST MILFORD JUNIOR HIGH

Brenda Davis walked up to the crowd gathered on the school's sidewalk. "Wow," she murmured, "it's still here."

Someone had spray-painted the word LOSERS! near the junior high's main entrance. The bright red letters really stood out against the pale gray stone of the building's front wall. Everyone had seen it that morning when they'd arrived for class. Now school was over, and the big red insult was still there.

Brenda sidled up to Jeremy Jefferson, a fellow seventh grader standing on the fringes of the group. "What's going on?" she asked him.

33

Like Brenda, Jeremy was tall for their age. He wore small, round wire-rimmed glasses, and was hardly ever seen without a cool Kangol cap or crazy-patterned pants.

Brenda liked bright colors too. She dyed her own cargo pants, shirts, and bandanas. Some of the people in her neighborhood admired them so much, she'd even started selling her creations.

"Hey, Brenda," he said. "I can't tell you what's going on. But I know what's coming off. Check it out." He jerked his thumb towards the school parking lot.

Brenda turned to see two men in overalls emerging from a municipal van. "Who are they?" she asked.

"They're from the city's graffiti clean-up crew," Jeremy informed her.

As the graffiti cleaners approached, Hal Turner stepped up to them. He was the student council president. "It's about time you got here," he declared. "That stupid word's been on the school since this morning!"

"Well, don't blame us," one of the men shrugged. "We couldn't clean a thing until the police made out their report."

Brenda remembered seeing the police car pull up to their school two hours before. She'd been daydreaming in history class, gazing out the window. But the police lights woke her up fast.

Spraying illegal graffiti was a serious crime in the city of Milford. Obviously, that hadn't stopped some vandal from defacing their junior high's front wall.

"Some jerk at East Milford must have done this!" exclaimed eighth grader Darla Kroll. "But *they're* the ones who are going to lose on Friday. Big time!"

Darla was the pep squad's head cheerleader. Around her, Darla's fellow cheerleaders shouted their agreement.

Brenda sighed. She could guess why Darla was blaming someone at East for doing this. In four days, the West Milford Wildcats were scheduled to play an important football game against the East Milford Eagles. But the rivalry between the two schools seemed like a friendly one to Brenda.

"It's hard to believe someone at East did this," she said. "A lot of us Westies hang out with Easties."

Darla turned her angry gaze on Brenda. "Are you talking about yourself, Brenda?"

Brenda shrugged. "Sure. There are a lot of nice kids that go to East. I met them through The Art Task Force."

So did Jeremy, for that matter. Both Brenda and Jeremy were serious art students, and they'd gotten to be pretty good friends working on community art projects.

Darla put her hands on her hips. "Well, Brenda, if you're such a big fan of *East* Milford Junior High, maybe you should sit with *their* pep squad on Friday."

"Straight up!" agreed Darla's fellow cheerleader Ashley Potter. "You tell her, Darla!"

"Yeah!" exclaimed some of the other girls.

Jeremy leaned in towards Brenda. "Don't let them get to you," he whispered. "Darla's being a total hypocrite."

"What do you mean?" Brenda asked.

Jeremy shrugged. "Darla was dating the East Milford Eagles star quarterback all summer long. Apparently, it was okay to like the Easties—until one of them dumped her."

Brenda raised an eyebrow at that. But it certainly

explained why Darla suddenly disliked East Milford Junior High so much.

"Move along now, kids," interrupted one of the men from the city. He and his partner had begun to unload their cleaning supplies from a carrying case. "We need to start working on this wall."

The knot of kids dispersed. Some headed up the sidewalk. Others moved to the corner to cross the street. The cheerleaders headed back into school for their practice.

Everyone left the area except Brenda and Jeremy. As art students, they wanted to see how the men were going to remove the paint without damaging the stone surface of the building.

"Let's watch from over there," Brenda suggested to Jeremy. She pointed across the street.

> TUESDAY, SEPTEMBER 25
> 3:30 P.M.
> WEST SIDE PARK

A city park was directly across from West Milford Junior High. Jeremy bought a hot dog and soda from a park vendor's cart. Brenda bought an ice cream bar. They carried their food to a bench. From there, they had a great view of the men working to clean the graffiti.

"What did the police do when they came?" Brenda

asked Jeremy, between bites of ice cream. "Do you know?"

Jeremy worked in the school office, so he pretty much knew everything that happened at West Milford. "The police took photos of the graffiti. Then they took a statement from the principal," Jeremy said after swallowing a big bite of hot dog. "And, I don't have to tell you, Principal Salis was pretty ticked off."

"Yeah, I know," Brenda replied. She'd heard just how angry Mr. Salis was when he spoke over the public address system that morning. He'd asked students to come forward with any ideas about who had defaced their school.

"Has anyone come forward yet?" Brenda asked.

Jeremy shrugged. "Not that I've heard."

Brenda continued to eat her ice cream. "You know what I wonder? Where did this vandal even get any spray paint?"

"I was wondering the same thing," Jeremy said. "Spray paint's about as rare in this town as Brazilian butterflies."

Two years ago, when city officials passed their strict anti-graffiti laws, they'd made it a crime to sell spray paint to anyone under the age of twenty-one. Retail stores and art teachers were required to keep spray paint in locked cabinets. Most stores in the city didn't even sell it anymore.

"You don't think this will hurt Mrs. Petit's plans for the next community project, do you?" Brenda asked.

"Why would it?" Jeremy replied.

"You know why. Team Twelve uses spray paint."

Mrs. Petit was the art teacher at East Milford Junior High. For three years, she'd been spearheading a fantastic public project called The Art Task Force, or "Team Twelve," as they sometimes called themselves.

Team Twelve consisted of the top six art students at East Milford and West Milford schools. They all worked together to create outdoor murals. It was a way to show off their talent while brightening up drab areas of the city with free public art.

This was the first year for Brenda and Jeremy to be on The Art Task Force. Since the new school year had begun a few weeks ago, they'd helped create a marine life mural on a warehouse wall near the city docks. They were scheduled to create more murals in the months to come.

"As long as nobody from Mrs. Petit's Art Task Force is involved, then it probably won't matter," Jeremy said.

"Good," Brenda replied. She finished her ice cream and wiped her hands with a napkin. Jeremy finished his hot dog and downed the last of his drink.

"If you're done with your soda, give it here," Brenda said.

Jeremy handed over the empty can and Brenda walked to the metal basket on the corner. It was the closet trashcan to the school for three blocks. As she tossed the garbage in, something caught her eye.

"Jeremy!" She waved frantically. "Get over here!"

Jeremy sighed and trudged to the corner. "What?"

"Look," Brenda said.

Behind his round, wire-rimmed glasses, Jeremy's eyes bulged like a bug's. "It can't be," he said.

"Oh, yes it can." Brenda shoved up her shirt sleeve and reached into the trash basket to pull out her discovery. "It's a can of red spray paint!"

```
TUESDAY, SEPTEMBER 25
4:20 P.M.
CORNER OF MAIN AND WEST PARK STREETS
```

"We have to take this evidence to the principal," Jeremy declared. He reached for the spray paint can, but Brenda pulled it away.

"In a minute, okay?" she said.

"Why?" Jeremy asked.

"Because…there might be clues to who did this on the can." She studied it closely. "Look," she said. "See the *Arial Aerosol* brand name running up its side? This is the same kind of spray paint we use on The Art Task Force to create outdoor murals."

"But that graffiti is legal," Jeremy pointed out. "Mrs. Petit gets permission for us to paint before we uncap the first can!"

"I know," Brenda said, turning the spray paint around in

her hand to examine it.

"What are you looking for?" Jeremy asked.

Brenda gasped. "Oh, no," she whispered.

Jeremy leaned in. On the bottom of the can, letters and numbers were written in black permanent marker.

EMJH Rm 221

"Oh, man," said Jeremy, shaking his head. "EMJH has to be East Milford Junior High."

"And Room 221 is East Milford's art room," Brenda added. "*EMJH Rm 221* is exactly how Mrs. Petit marks all of her art supplies."

Jeremy shook his head. "I really feel sorry for Mrs. P."

"Why?" Brenda asked.

"What do you mean *why*?" Jeremy threw up his hands. "Principal Salis is going to blame her when he sees this."

"Blame her for what?!" Brenda replied. "You don't think a teacher would spray illegal graffiti, do you?"

"No," Jeremy said. "But Mrs. Petit is responsible for the spray paint in her closet. She's supposed to keep it

41

locked up, yet she let one of her students have this paint."

"There could be another explanation," Brenda protested.

"It's not our business," Jeremy said. "We should just take the can to the principal and let him sort it out." Jeremy reached for the can again. Once again, Brenda pulled it away.

"But he's angry," she argued. "And justice is supposed to be fair and without passion. So maybe we should sort it out first."

"Have you gone *mental*? The police are already involved and—" Jeremy abruptly stopped talking. He gaped at the can in silence.

"What?" Brenda asked. "What's your problem?"

"It's not my problem, Brenda," he said. "It's yours. You've already put your fingerprints all over that can."

"What are you talking about?" Brenda's asked in horror. "You don't think they'll accuse me, do you?"

"No," Jeremy said. "But you probably messed up any fingerprints that might have been on there."

Brenda frowned. She hadn't even thought of that.

TUESDAY, SEPTEMBER 25
4:35 P.M.
WEST MILFORD JR. HIGH
PRINCIPAL'S OFFICE

"I'm not arguing with you anymore," Jeremy said. Let's go talk to the principal. *Now*."

42

"Sorry, Jeremy, but Mr. Salis is gone for the day," said Mrs. Keppler, one of the school secretaries. "He had a meeting at city center. Whatever you needed to see him about will have to wait until tomorrow morning."

Jeremy left the office. He found Brenda waiting for him on a bench outside. "Let's go," he told her. "Principal Salis is gone for the day."

Brenda nodded. She patted her backpack, where she'd put the spray paint can. "I'll just stash it in my locker," she said as they walked down the empty hall. "We can talk to the principal together in the morning."

Jeremy shook his head. "It'll have to be the afternoon. I've got a dentist's appointment."

"Some people have all the fun," Brenda teased.

"Don't even joke about it," he said, pointing to his mouth. "I've got three cavities."

"Okay," Brenda said, "see you tomorrow afternoon then."

As Jeremy headed toward the school's front doors, Brenda walked down the long hall to her locker. She opened her backpack and took another look at the spray can.

Curious to see whether all the paint was used up, she pulled out her notebook and shook the can. The shaker beads rolled around loudly. She depressed the nozzle. A tiny bit of paint came out, enough to make a fat streak across the front of her notebook, but not much else.

"I guess painting *LOSERS* took it all out of you," she murmured to the can. Then, with a shrug, Brenda recapped the paint and shoved it onto her locker shelf.

```
Tuesday, September 25
4:45 p.m.
West Milford Jr. High Hallway
```

Ashley Potter was super thirsty. She'd totally drained her water bottle during cheerleading practice. So after Darla Kroll called the end of practice and everyone rushed for the gym's exit, Ashley ducked back into the school hallway.

She'd been standing at the water fountain, taking a long drink, when she heard a rattling sound—like a paint can being shaken.

Ashley crept down a short hall and peeked around the corner. Just a few feet away, she saw that gangly, tie-dyeing freak Brenda Davis standing in front of her locker, shaking a red paint can.

Ashley's jaw dropped. She not only saw Brenda spray a streak of red paint on her own notebook, but she heard her say something about using all the paint in the spray can to create the *LOSERS* graffiti.

Ohmigosh, Ashley thought, as she watched Brenda stash the paint can in her locker. *Now I know who spray painted our front wall!*

"But I *am* telling the truth," Brenda insisted the next morning. "I didn't vandalize the school."

Principal Salis was red-faced. He pounded his desk with his fist. "You're lying!"

This was the second morning graffiti had appeared at West Milford Junior High. The night before, the vandal had defaced the Wildcats sign hanging on the playing field fence. Brenda had seen it on her way into school. It read:

MR. SALIS

East Eagles Forever! Number 10 Rules!

The words were painted in the very same red spray paint that had been used to paint *LOSERS!* the night before.

"Need I remind you again of the overwhelming evidence against you, Ms. Davis?" Principal Salis asked from his big leather desk chair. "We found this red spray paint can in your locker."

He held up the *Arial Aerosol* can she'd found with Jeremy the day before.

"We also found the exact same type of can at the scene of last night's vandalism near the football field fence," the principal continued. He held up a second *Arial Aerosol* can. "We even found your history notebook with a test streak of red paint on the cover." He held that up too. "And after I turn the can recovered from your locker over to the police, I'm sure we'll find your fingerprints on it, won't we?"

"But I've explained all that, and—" Brenda said.

"Yes, I know," Mr. Salis interrupted. "You claim that you found the can in the trash basket across the street."

"Just ask Jeremy Jefferson," Brenda pleaded.

Mr. Salis shook his head. "Mr. Jefferson isn't here this morning, Ms. Davis, and I know you two are friends. So anything he claims will be taken with a grain of salt."

"What do you mean by that?" Brenda asked.

"In my experience, friends lie to protect each other all the time," he replied.

"But Jeremy's not that kind of person," Brenda said. "He'll tell you what really happened."

"Then he better have proof, because I have a witness. One of the cheerleading squad overheard you confess in the hall!"

"What?!" Brenda cried.

"Oh, yes," said the principal. "You must have thought the hall was deserted, but one of the cheerleaders overheard you mumble something about painting the graffiti. That's who turned you in this morning."

"But why would I do it?" Brenda countered desperately. "I go to West Milford! Why would I paint anything bad about it?"

The principal sighed. "My witness tells me that you have a lot of friends at East Milford, so I can easily see your motivation. You were trying to impress your friends on the East Side."

"I can't believe this is happening," Brenda murmured.

"Well, Ms. Davis, you better believe it. Your Art Task Force days are over. And, as of this moment, you're suspended for a week. Your parents and the police will be notified by the end of the day. As you well know, this is a criminal matter."

◇◇◇◇◇◇◇◇◇◇◇◇

For hours after her disastrous meeting with the principal, Brenda tried to contact Jeremy Jefferson. But his cell phone didn't pick up. Finally, she called his home.

Mrs. Jefferson answered. Apparently, Jeremy was having a bad reaction to the anesthetic the dentist had given him.

He was sleeping all afternoon, and he wasn't coming back to school today.

Great, Brenda thought. *Looks like I'm on my own for now.*

She'd gone straight home after being suspended, but her mother was out shopping. So she fixed herself some lunch, and then decided to take a chance. She caught a crosstown bus to Milford's East Side.

```
WEDNESDAY, SEPTEMBER 26
3:05 P.M.
EAST MILFORD JUNIOR HIGH, MAIN ENTRANCE
```

The school day had just ended. Most of the East Milford students were rushing for the exit. Brenda felt like a salmon swimming upstream as she plowed her way into the building.

"Hey, Brenda, is that you?"

Just inside the crowded doorway, Brenda saw a familiar face approaching her. Sophia Benedict had big brown eyes and honey-brown hair she wore in a ponytail. Brenda had met her through The Art Task Force. She was a year older than Brenda, however, so this was her second year on "Team Twelve."

"What are you doing over on the East side?" Sophia asked.

Trying to find out who really *spray-painted* LOSERS! *on West Milford's front wall,* Brenda wanted to say, but didn't.

Instead she said, "I need to talk with Mrs. Petit."

"I'll walk you to her classroom," Sophia offered. "She's bound to be there. Wednesday is her day for catching up with grading artwork. What's up?"

"I'd rather not say," Brenda replied.

"*Oh*. Okay, then," Sophia said with a frown.

Brenda felt the chill, but she knew Sophia was a big gossip. Word about Brenda's suspension—and the reason for it—was bound to spread to East Milford. But Brenda wasn't going to help it along! As far as she was concerned, the only person who needed to know she'd been accused of vandalism was Mrs. Petit.

The East Milford art room was on the second floor, Room 221, just like the markings on the bottom of the spray paint cans. As Sophia walked Brenda toward the north staircase, they passed the East Milford gymnasium. The big double doors suddenly burst open in front of them. Two dozen boys filed out toward an exit that led to the football field. Brenda and Sophia had to wait until they passed.

As the football numbers flew by Brenda, she recognized a few of them. Number 8 was eighth grader Timothy Burr. He was one of the most talented kids on The Art Task Force. He waved at Sophia and Brenda. They waved back.

Brenda also recognized Number 10. He was the team's star quarterback—Parker Robertson.

"Parker!" called a pretty girl in a cheerleading outfit. She raced down the hall, her long, straw blond hair flying behind her. "Here's my new cell number. Don't forget to call me when practice is over."

"Sure, Sunny," said Parker, folding the number and stuffing it into his sweatpants pocket.

Sophia leaned close to Brenda. "That's Sue Lane," she whispered. "'Sunny' is her nickname. She and Parker have been going out since the start of the school year."

Brenda remembered what Jeremy said about Parker Robertson dumping Darla Kroll from their school. Now Brenda knew the reason—"Sunny" Sue Lane.

Parker probably figured it was a lot more convenient to date a cheerleader from his own school, Brenda thought. Then she focused in on his jersey number again.

Number 10.

Wait, she thought. *Isn't that the same number that was on this morning's graffiti? "East Eagles Forever! Number 10 rules!"*

Brenda suddenly wondered if Sunny Sue Lane had anything to do with the graffiti. Maybe she was trying to help Parker psych out the West Milford Wildcats before the big game.

Or maybe Darla was still competing for Parker's attention. And maybe Sunny wanted to rub it in that Parker was her boyfriend now and Darla was the Loser.

Or maybe Parker himself had sprayed the graffiti. Brenda didn't know much about him. Maybe he was a really nasty competitor and was into dissing his opponents.

Brenda would have kept thinking this over, but she was interrupted by Sophia.

"Look," she whispered, tugging on Brenda's shirt. "There's my crush."

"Hey, Doug!" she called out loudly to a cute boy wearing a Number 12 Eagles jersey. "Good luck on Friday!"

"Thanks!" he replied as he jogged by.

"I think Doug is *soooo* cute," Sophia whispered. "He's so popular and so smart. I think he's as good a quarterback as Parker Robertson."

"Uh-huh," Brenda mumbled as they finally climbed the north staircase. She was only half-listening to Sophia's gossip. Brenda was too worried about her own problems.

"Doug's pretty annoyed the coach has him playing second string," Sophia rambled on. "The only way he'll ever get to start a game is if Parker can't play. I wish I could get his attention, but I heard a rumor he's secretly dating Darla Kroll. She's from your school. Do you know her?"

"Not really," Brenda said. But now she began to wonder about Darla. *Could she have sprayed "Number 10 Rules!" to make it look like Parker Robertson had sprayed it? Was Darla trying to get Parker in trouble, to get back at him for dumping her at the start of the school year?*

Or could Doug Jones be the vandal? Brenda asked herself. *It sounded like he really wanted to play Parker's position. Could he be the one trying to set Parker up?*

And what about Sophia? Brenda wondered. *She did say she was crushing on Doug. Maybe she was trying to win points with him by dissing his West Side rivals in living color.*

The second floor was much less crowded than the first. Only a few students were still hanging by their lockers. Walking toward the art room, Brenda recognized a girl with black hair and heavy black eyeliner.

Kari Sky was another member of "Team Twelve." Black was her favorite color. She was usually dressed in it—and today was no exception. She wore black boots, a long black skirt, and a black sweater.

"Hi, Kari," Sophia called as they passed her.

Kari nodded neutrally at Sophia. But when she moved her gaze to Brenda, she frowned and glared.

"What's her problem?" Brenda whispered. "She was like that when we worked on the marine mural, too. She didn't say a word to me or Jeremy. Just glared at us."

Sophia shrugged. "Kari doesn't like kids from West Milford."

"Why not?"
Brenda asked.

"She used to
live on your side of
town," Sophia
explained. "They
didn't get her Goth
thing, you know?
And she got
teased a lot."

"Oh," Brenda
said, glancing back
over her shoulder.
Kari was still glaring at her. *Yikes.*

"Well, anyway, here we are," Sophia announced. "This

is Mrs. Petit's classroom here."

The door to 221 was closed. Brenda peeked through the window. Just as Sophia had said, Mrs. Petit was sitting at her desk, grading art projects.

Brenda knocked.

"Brenda? What are you doing here?" Mrs. Petit asked when she answered the door.

"I need to speak with you," Brenda explained. "It's sort of urgent."

"Oh? Okay." The art teacher held the door open. She noticed Sophia lingering in the hall. "Do you need something Sophia?" she called.

"No, Mrs. Petit," she said. "I was, uh...just leaving."

The teacher closed the door again. "Now what's this all about?"

Brenda took a deep breath. "I've got a *lot* to tell you, Mrs. Petit," she said. "And I really need your help."

> WEDNESDAY, SEPTEMBER 26
> 3:45 P.M.
> EMJH, Room 221

Brenda explained everything that had happened since the day before—the vandalism, finding the can of red spray paint, being wrongly accused. Mrs. Petit was horrified to hear the details.

"I want to help you, Brenda," said Mrs. Petit, sitting at her desk in the art room. "And I'm happy to vouch for you. But the best defense we can give you is to find the person who actually did the vandalism."

"That's what I thought, too," said Brenda. She was sitting beside Mrs. Petit in a chair pulled from one of the room's many art tables. "That's why I came to you. Did you give red spray paint to any of your students?"

"No," Mrs. Petit said. Then she sighed. "But now I know what happened to at least two of my five missing spray paint cans."

"Missing?" Brenda asked. "Or stolen?"

"I restocked my supply closet on Monday morning at ten o'clock," Mrs. Petit explained.

She pointed to the door behind her desk. Brenda noticed a padlock on the outside of it.

"But when I checked the closet at noon," Mrs. Petit continued, "some cans were missing. I counted up the inventory and came up with a total of five cans missing."

Brenda's eyes widened with excitement. *Now we're getting somewhere!* she thought. "Who had access to the supply closet between ten and noon on Monday?" she asked the teacher.

"Only one eighth grade class had access to that closet. This is their artwork, here. They just completed their work during this morning's class, and I was in the middle of grading it when you knocked on the door." She pointed to a stack of paintings on her desk.

Brenda picked up a few of the colorful paintings. "These were done in watercolor, not spray paint."

"That's right," said Mrs. Petit. "And the watercolor supplies were already on the art tables when the class began on  Monday and again this morning. There was no reason for anyone to enter the closet behind me."

"So *who* went into your supply closet?" Brenda asked. "You must have seen the person. They had to walk right by your desk!"

When I'm out of the art room, I always padlock that closet. During class, I'm here, so there's no need to keep it locked.

"Ok, but I still don't get it. If the closet was unlocked,

then you were still in the classroom. So you must have seen the person who stole the paints, right?"

"Wrong," Mrs. Petit confessed. "I stepped out of class to take an important phone call. I was only gone ten minutes, but that's the only time it could have happened."

"Then somebody in that class must have seen who took the paints," Brenda concluded.

Mrs. Petit nodded. "That same group of students meets Mondays, Wednesdays, and Fridays. So when I had them again this morning, I asked who took the paints. They all just stared at me, unfortunately."

"Nobody wanted to look like a tattletale, right?" Brenda said.

"Right. Nobody would confess, and nobody would tell on a fellow student. Of course, I didn't press them too hard. But things are different now...you're facing real penalties if we can't get to the bottom of who stole the paint and vandalized West Milford."

"Can you tell me the names of the kids in that class?" Brenda asked.

"You have them right there." The teacher pointed to the stack of watercolor paintings. "Students print their names on the back of their artwork."

Brenda borrowed a piece of paper from Mrs. Petit and jotted down all the names in her eighth grade class. She put them in alphabetical order. Then she studied the list. She underlined any names she already knew and made short notes beside each name.

-<u>Sophia Benedict</u>-on Team Twelve, likes to gossip, has a crush on Doug Jones

-<u>Timothy Burr</u>-on Team Twelve, great art student, #08 on football team

-<u>Andy Comacho</u>-? Don't Know

-<u>Able Green</u>-? DK

-<u>Doug Jones</u>-2nd string quarterback, #12 on football team, dating Darla Kroll?

-<u>Sunny Sue Lane</u>-dating Parker Robertson, East Milford cheerleader

-<u>Anson O'Rourke</u>-? DK

-<u>Parker Robertson</u>-star quarterback, dumped Darla for Sunny, #10 on team

-<u>Maria Sellers</u>-? DK

-<u>Kari Sky</u>-on Team Twelve, loves black, hates anyone from West Milford

-<u>Thom Yardley</u>-? DK

As Brenda looked at the list, an idea occurred to her. "I'll tell you the truth, Mrs. Petit. If I were in your class, there's no way I would have the nerve to tell on someone in front of all the other students."

"That's natural," Mrs. Petit admitted.

"But I'd also feel guilty for not helping you," Brenda added.

"What are you getting at?" Mrs. Petit asked.

"I'd probably try to find some quiet way of telling you the truth. Did someone pass you a note after class this morning?"

Mrs. Petit shook her head. "The only thing the class passed me was their artwork."

Brenda scratched her head in thought. Then she started looking more closely at the watercolor paintings.

No one had written anything on the backs of the paintings—except their names, of course. There were no extra notes or hints as to who might have stolen the spray paint.

But one painting looked really odd to Brenda.

"This artwork isn't very good at all," she noticed.

"I know. It's terrible," Mrs. Petit said. "It's not like Timothy Burr to do such awful work. He's one of my very best students."

Brenda nodded. "I met him when we painted the marine life mural near the docks. He out-painted Kari, Sophia, Jeremy, and me. He was the best of Team Twelve by far!"

Brenda looked again at Timothy's painting. It featured a giant eagle. One clawed foot gripped a football. The other grasped a half-dozen paint brushes dripping with different colored paints. The eagle flew over a giant football field. In the background, a billboard rose up. The sign displayed an array of letters and numbers, dripping with paint. It looked as if the eagle had just used his many-colored brushes to paint the billboard.

"Wait a second! East Milford Eagles! Paint brushes! I think Tim Burr is trying to tell you something here."

The teacher looked again at the painting. "You're right. His theme suggests East Milford Eagles football. Does that mean one of the football players in my class stole the paint?"

"But which player? And why?" Brenda wondered aloud. Then she remembered something from an art lesson. "Wait! Look here. I think Tim is using a color trick I learned back in sixth grade."

Brenda pointed to the billboard in Tim's painting—the sign that was covered in letters and numbers.

"What trick?" Mrs. Petit asked.

"You see how the letters and numbers are all different colors? Well, if you place a color filter over them, then you block out certain colors and—"

"Oh, yes. I see!" Mrs. Petit cried. "It's a way of coding a message!"

Brenda and Mrs. Petit went to the art supply closet. They pulled out every color of cellophane paper they could get their hands on. Blue, green yellow, orange...they tried overlaying each color on Tim's painting. Finally, they tried the red.

Brenda gasped. "Look at that! Now we know who stole the paints!"

Can you solve the Case of the Innocent Art Student?

Look at the color-coded message that was in Timothy Burr's artwork. Can you figure out who stole the paints and painted the illegal graffiti? Check the U-Solve-It! *web site to see if you're right!*

The Case of the Suspicious Spelling Bee

1. THE FINAL WORD

Eleven-year-old Sara Bishop adjusted her rectangular glasses and took a deep breath.

"Are you ready?" Mr. Fisher asked.

Standing on the vast sports arena stage, Sara exhaled and nodded.

"Your word is *antipyretic*," Mr. Fisher said.

Uh-oh, Sara thought. *That's not a word I've spelled before.*

For Sara, that was a pretty big deal. She'd been entering school spelling bees for five years. For the last three, she'd actually made it to the regional finals. But this was the first year she'd studied hard enough and long enough to come this close to first place.

For over two hours now, she'd been flawlessly spelling some very difficult words. She hadn't gotten one word wrong yet. The twenty-five kids sitting on chairs behind her were representing twenty-five elementary and junior high schools from all over the Fairfield region. One by one, each of them had misspelled a word. One by one, each of them had fallen out of the competition.

Now it was down to Sara and an older girl. The two of them had been spelling words in a one-on-one spell-off for fifteen minutes now.

"Definition, please, sir?" Sara asked.

Mr. Fisher nodded. He glanced at the 3 x 5 card in his hand. "An *antipyretic* is an agent that reduces fever," he said.

Perfect, Sara thought. *I could use an antipyretic about now!*

She felt warm enough to be feverish on this huge stage. Hot lights were beating down from above. And her mouth felt drier than a wad of cotton.

Sara tried not to look out into the audience. Half the state had shown up to watch the regional finals. And if that weren't distracting enough, giant video screens were hanging all over the arena. When they weren't broadcasting flashy multimedia graphics, they were showing her image thirty feet high. It totally freaked Sara out.

"Go, Sara!" yelled a young kid in the front row.

Sara froze in embarrassment. The cheer had come from her five-year-old sister, Nina. She was sitting with Sara's family right up front. Her little cheer echoed in the big arena.

The super-quiet crowd began to titter with laughter.

Just then, Sara noticed a young blond man rushing over to the little girl. His lanky form was dressed in the official outfit of the arena's employees—a navy blue blazer and khaki pants. Over his sandy blond hair, he wore a broadcaster's headset.

Sara could see the young blond man was asking Nina to remain quiet. Then he turned and gave a hand signal to someone on the stage.

"Whenever you're ready, Sara," Mr. Fisher said.

Sara cleared her throat and focused. "Antipyretic," she repeated, trying to keep the shakiness out of her voice. She closed her eyes and tried to picture writing her word on a blackboard. "A-N-T-I ..."

That seems obvious enough, she thought. *Now for the hard part.*

"...P-I-R-E-T-I-C. Antipyretic," she finished.

"I'm sorry," Mr. Fisher said. "But that's incorrect."

The entire audience released a *whoosh* of disappointed breath. But no one was more disappointed than Sara.

It's not over yet, she told herself as she made her way back to her folding chair. *The other girl could still mess up, too.*

But fourteen-year-old Charlotte "Cha-Cha" Hartman didn't mess up. As she'd done all night long, she strode coolly up to the microphone. Like a beauty pageant contestant,

Cha-Cha looked totally poised and perfect. There wasn't one drop of sweat on her pretty forehead.

She wasn't shy about looking out into the audience. Like she always did, she flipped back her bouncy red tresses and gave a little wave to a teenage boy sitting in the front row.

Cha-Cha's friend had shaggy brown hair with white-blond streaks. He wore a colorful shirt with letters all over it. He threw Charlotte what looked like elaborate peace-out and thumbs-up signs.

"Are you ready, Charlotte?" Mr. Fisher asked.

"Cha-Cha is ready to Cha-Cha!" Charlotte sang out for the umpteenth time that night.

"What does she think this is?" whispered the twelve-year-old boy sitting next to Sara. "*American Idol*?"

Sara glanced at the boy. He rolled his eyes. Charlotte Hartman hadn't just come to *spell* tonight. That was clear enough. She'd come to make a splash.

She'd dressed in bright red from head to toe. Her dress was covered in hearts. A big heart necklace hung around her neck. And heart-shaped glasses graced the tip of her upturned nose. The whole outfit was obviously a way for everyone to remember her last name: *Hartman*.

"All right, then, Cha-Cha!" Mr. Fisher said with a big smile. "Your word is *pococurante*."

2. AND THE LOSER IS...

"Tough luck, Sara," called some kids from her elementary school as they headed towards the shadowy parking lot.

"Yeah, too bad."

"Better luck next year!"

Sara stood beneath the lighted archway of the sports arena's entrance with her mother; her little sister, Nina; and her older cousin, Keith. The family's mini-van was parked pretty far away, so her dad and uncle told them all to wait until they brought the vehicle around.

I should have gone with my dad, Sara thought, as more and more people she knew from school walked by. But she didn't say it. She didn't want to cry either. *Just because I feel like a total loser, doesn't mean I have to act like it!*

With a stiff smile firmly in place, Sara waved and nodded to her classmates as they filed past her. Through gritted teeth, she whispered to her cousin, "What's the world's record for keeping a fake smile frozen on your face?"

"I don't know," Keith replied. "But I'm betting Cha-Cha wins that one too. She wore that plastic, beauty pageant smirk for the entire bee—two hours and twenty minutes. That's got to be some kind of record."

Keith Bishop was fourteen. He was Sara's first cousin and a really nice guy. For the past few months, Sara's parents had hired him to baby-sit Sara and Nina on Friday nights. So Sara had gotten to know him pretty well.

"Hey, Keith, what are you doing here?"

Sara turned to see a teenage girl walking up to them. She had ink black braids, big green eyes, and a dimpled smile.

"I never thought I'd see you at the Fairfield arena for anything but basketball," the girl said with a laugh.

Keith shook his head. "Tonight I came to cheer for my cousin." He gestured to Sara. "Beni Wilcox, this is Sara Bishop."

"So you're Keith's cousin?" Beni asked brightly. "I should have figured you were related from your last names."

Sara nodded, still valiantly struggling to keep her fake smile in place.

"You should be proud of yourself," Beni told her. "I

thought you did really well tonight. You hung tough for an incredibly long time."

But not long enough, Sara thought miserably. *In the end, I blew it.*

Beni held up an expensive video camera. "I filmed the whole thing for Charlotte Hartman."

"For Charlotte?" Keith asked in confusion.

Beni nodded. "Yeah, she's paying me and everything. If you want, I can make a copy for you guys, too. I'll just charge you for the cost of the tape."

Sure, that's all I need, Sara thought, *a video to watch myself crash and burn over and over again.*

"That's nice of you, Beni," Keith quickly replied when he saw Sara's tense expression. "We'll get back to you, okay?"

"Sure, okay. See you," Beni called as she walked away.

Sara finally let her frozen smile melt. She turned to her cousin. "Who was that girl again?"

"Benita Wilcox," Keith said. "She goes to my junior high. I saw her filming our spelling bee, too. But I thought it was a school project, because she's always filming stuff for Union's video yearbook. I didn't know Charlotte hired her."

"Do you know Charlotte, too, then?" Sara asked. "I mean, since she goes to your school."

"I'm in two classes with her," Keith admitted. "But I'm not a friend or anything, and…"

Keith's voice trailed off. "And what?" Sara pressed.

"And I'm surprised she won, that's all. She never struck me as very smart. She almost never has her homework done. Until now, all she seemed to care about was Drama Club and Chorus, not spelling."

"Well, I've been in these finals for three years straight," Sara said, "and I lost every time. This is Charlotte's first time here, and she won. So she must be some kind of secret genius."

"There she is now," Keith whispered.

He pointed to a red convertible sports car in the nearby employee parking area. Standing beside it, Cha-Cha Hartman squealed and gave a high-five to a boy her age with streaked, shaggy hair.

Sara recognized the boy. He'd been sitting in the front row during the bee. He was still wearing that wacky "spelling bee" shirt with colorful letters all over it.

"There she is! There's my Cha-Cha!" The exclamation came from a beefy, balding older man. He strode up to Charlotte. "You did it," the man told Cha-Cha. "Five thousand dollars and a trip to D.C. Congratulations, baby!"

"Thanks, Daddy!" Cha-Cha replied.

That's when Sara realized the big, balding man was Charlotte Hartman's father. She also noticed what he was wearing—a navy blue blazer, khaki pants, and a Fairfield Sports Arena baseball cap.

Now Sara knew why she hadn't seen Mr. Hartman sitting in the front rows with the families of the other contestants. He was an employee of the Fairfield Sports Arena, and he'd been working during the bee.

Just then, Sara noticed another man walking into the employee parking lot. "Goodnight, Mr. Hartman," the man called to Charlotte's father with a wave.

"Phil, wait!" Mr. Hartman jogged over to the young man.

As the two men moved into a pool of light, Sara saw that the newcomer was the same young blond employee who'd rushed over to Sara's family and asked her little sister to remain quiet. He wasn't wearing his headset anymore—no surprise. He'd replaced it with a Fairfield Sports Arena ball cap like the one Mr. Hartman was wearing. But he was still wearing his official navy blazer and khaki pants.

Mr. Hartman reached into his own blazer and handed the younger man an envelope. The younger man nodded. Then he unlocked his SUV, climbed inside, and drove away.

Cha-Cha's father returned to his daughter and they began to pile into his red convertible. "Aren't you excited?" he crowed. "Now it's on to Washington and national television!"

Still waiting by the arena's entryway, Sara watched Cha-Cha laugh as she rode away. Sara tensed, fighting the urge to dissolve into tears. She'd worked so hard this year to win these regional finals. It was a tough blow to come so close and watch someone else win.

"I'm thirsty!" Sara's little sister suddenly cried.

"I know, Nina," their mom said. "Daddy's coming with the car. There's Ruby Juice in the back."

"Ruby Juice! Ruby Juice!" Nina chanted as she danced around.

Sara rolled her eyes. She wished she was five again, when all it took to cheer you up was a bottle of Ruby Juice.

3. A MYSTERIOUS MESSAGE

A few days later, Sara was doing her homework when her mom entered her bedroom.

"A letter came for you," she said.

"A letter?" Sara said. "For me?"

Her mom handed it to her and left the room again.

Sara stared at the letter and scratched her head. Nobody sent real letters anymore. She got cards from her grandparents. But these days everyone she knew wrote letters in e-mail, not snail mail.

Sara's name and address were typed on the front. But she didn't see a return address. Three raised gold letters were printed where a return address should have been.

"FSA," she whispered. "Who could this be from? I don't know anyone with those initials."

Sara opened the envelope. Inside was a clean, white sheet of paper. The same three raised gold initials were printed at the top. And in the middle of the vast, white sheet there were only two words:

Cha-Cha cheated.

4. A SECOND OPINION

Before Sara showed the note to her parents, she wanted someone else's opinion on it.

Her cousin Keith Bishop lived only two streets away. It was a short walk to his house. When Sara got there, she found him in his front drive, shooting baskets.

"'Cha-Cha cheated,'" Keith read aloud after Sara handed him the mysterious note. He stood with the note in one hand and a basketball in the other.

"You said you knew Cha-Cha Hartman," Sara said. "Do you think this note is bogus?"

"I don't know," Keith said. "Like I told you the other night, Charlotte Hartman is far from a brain in class. And she never cared about spelling bees before. But if she cheated, I can't see how she did it."

"Me, neither," Sara said.

"And if it is true, she certainly couldn't have cheated without help," Keith said. Still studying the note, he tucked the basketball under his arm, crossed the driveway, and sat on his front steps. "How Cha-Cha cheated and who may have helped her aren't the only mysteries here."

"You mean the note, right?" Sara said, sitting down beside him. "Who sent it and why?"

Keith nodded. "Do you have the envelope this came in?"

Sara pulled the envelope from her jeans pocket. Keith examined the back and front. "FSA," he read, running his fingers over the raised gold letters on the envelope.

"Those are the same initials at the top of the anonymous note. See." Sara pointed out the letters at the top of the paper. The trouble is…I don't know anyone with the initials FSA. Do you?"

"I don't think these are initials," Keith said.

Sara frowned. "What else would they be?"

"A logo," Keith said. "It's like a trademark or brand. This looks like pre-printed stationery, the kind businesses use. And you know what? I think I've seen this 'FSA' design before."

Sara sat up straight. "You have?"

"Come on inside," Keith said, rising from the front steps. "I want to check something out."

Keith was a big fan of college and pro basketball. Posters of his favorite players covered his bedroom walls. He even had a hoop over his door. When they got to Keith's room, he rifled through his stack of sports magazines and pulled out a thin glossy booklet.

"Sixth Annual Collegiate Exhibition," Sara read on the front cover of the booklet. Beneath it was a photo of a basketball player jumping high off the floor.

"What is this?" Sara asked.

"It's a program from this year's college basketball all-star tournament," Keith explained.

Sara put a hand on her hip. "Excuse me, but what does basketball have to do with spelling?"

"Look." Keith opened the booklet. Tucked inside was a special note of welcome to the all-star game audience. At the top of the note were three raised gold letters.

"FSA!" Sara cried. She snatched the note and compared it to the one she'd gotten today in the mail. "It's the exact same logo."

"Fairfield Sports Arena," Keith informed her. "Whoever sent you that anonymous note must work for the arena."

Sara shook her head and plopped down onto Keith's desk chair. "I don't get this!"

"If Cha-Cha cheated, then you should have won," Keith said as he began collecting the sponge basketballs scattered all over his floor. "So somebody at the sports arena thought you got ripped off. That's why you got the note. Do you know anyone who works at the arena?"

"No," Sara said.

"Neither do I—" Keith said.

"Wait a second," Sara interrupted. "Do you remember the night of the spelling bee, when we were waiting for my dad to bring the mini-van around?"

"Yeah?" Keith stopped collecting sponge balls and straightened up. "Oh, right! I know what you're going to say! Charlotte's father works at the arena. That's why we saw her waiting in the employee parking lot."

"Right," Sara said. "That's also why her dad was wearing an official sports arena blazer. But why would Charlotte's *father* send a note like this? It makes no sense for him to tell on his own daughter."

"You're right," Keith said. "Her dad looked happy that she'd won."

Sara sighed. "Maybe somebody's just playing a trick on me."

Keith thought that over. "You could be right," he said. "But the trick's not on you. Somebody could be angry at Cha-Cha and trying to get back at her—or her father."

Sara nodded. "That's probably what it is. I mean, the note doesn't say *how* Charlotte cheated or *who* may have helped her. Why would a person write a note like this and not tell me that too?"

Keith scratched his head. "What if this person who wrote the note doesn't know how she did it? Maybe this person saw something suspicious but couldn't figure out the details."

Sara threw up her hands. "But if I can't figure out how Charlotte cheated, then I'll just look ridiculous accusing her because of some crank note that I could have written myself!"

Keith sat down on his bed with his collection of sponge basketballs. He began making shot after shot at the hoop on his door. A minute later, he stopped shooting.

"Dex," he said.

"What?" Sara asked.

"Not *what*. Who. Dexter Adams is Charlotte Hartman's closest friend. I saw him in the audience the night of the regional finals."

"Was he the boy who wore that wacky spelling bee shirt?" Sara asked. "The one with all those different colored letters on it?"

"Yeah." Keith nodded. "Dex wore a shirt exactly like that when Charlotte won the bee at our junior high assembly."

"Was he sitting in the front row then, too?" Sara asked.

Keith nodded again.

"Maybe Dexter helped her cheat," Sara speculated. "But how exactly?"

"Keith!" a deep voice called from the other room. "We're

leaving in fifteen minutes!"

"That's your dad, isn't it?" Sara asked.

Keith checked his watch. "We're going to a game tonight at the Fairfield Arena. Listen, why don't you come with us? My dad can call your parents to let them know. Maybe going back there will jog a memory for you."

Sara nodded. "I guess it's worth a try."

5. ARENA ANSWERS

An hour later, Sara, Keith, and Mr. Bishop were sitting in the sports arena stands. They had a great view of the basketball court. Thousands of fans surrounded them. Giant multimedia screens flashed close-ups of the players. But Sara wasn't watching the game. She was thinking back to the night of the spelling bee.

Did Cha-Cha cheat? How did she do it? And who helped her if she did?

"It must have been her friend, Dexter," Sara murmured to herself. "He was the only one close enough to the stage... unless there was someone else..."

Sara tried to remember whether Cha-Cha's father had been near the stage that night. She couldn't recall seeing him, but then she hadn't looked into the audience very often.

I wonder where exactly Mr. Hartman works in this arena, she thought, turning in her seat to take in the huge space.

Keith's dad noticed Sara craning her neck. "What are you looking at, Sara?" He laughed and pointed to the court below them. "The game's down there."

Keith shot Sara a questioning look.

She leaned close and whispered in his ear. "I'm going to look around." Before Keith could stop her, she stood up. "I'll be back soon, Uncle Fred," she announced. "I have to use the restroom."

"Okay," Keith's dad replied.

Sara quickly left the stands and approached the escalator. She was currently on Level E. She took the escalator down four levels to Level A, the main floor.

A small "Information" booth stood near the ticket gate. Sara took a deep breath for courage and approached the woman sitting behind its counter. Her nametag read, "Ms. Ferris."

"Excuse me, Ms. Ferris," Sara began. "I have a message for Mr. Hartman, but I don't know where he works. Can you tell me where I can find him?"

"You can give me the message, honey," the woman said.

"No. It's, uh…from my father," Sara said. "He wanted me to talk directly to Mr. Hartman."

Ms. Ferris shook her head. "Mr. Hartman is in the control booth. He can't be disturbed during a game."

Sara's eyes widened. "The control booth? He works in the arena's control booth?"

"Yes, honey, he manages it," Ms. Ferris said. "Of course, he might not be doing that much longer."

"Why not?" Sara asked.

Ms. Ferris laughed. "Oh, I'm sure he's just joking about that. His daughter won a spot in the national spelling bee. He says once Hollywood agents see his baby on television, she'll be getting all sorts of offers to be in movies and TV shows, and he'll be moving to California with her."

Just then, the booth's phone rang. The woman answered it. "Just a moment, please. I'm helping a little girl—"

"Um…that's okay!" Sara said, quickly edging away. "I'll tell my dad what you said. Thanks!"

Sara walked along the main corridor until she found a map of the arena. She studied the line drawing, locating the control booth. "Level F," she whispered. "That's only one level above my uncle's seats."

She checked her watch as she rode the escalator back up. She'd been gone about seven minutes so far. She figured she had ten more before her uncle would start to look for her.

6. EMPLOYEES ONLY

When Sara arrived on Level F, she glanced around the floor. Dozens of basketball fans were wandering in and out of the seating area. They headed for the restrooms or stood online at the refreshment counter.

Sara dodged the wandering crowd until she came to a steel door. The sign on it read Control Booth, Employees Only. About ten feet away, two security guards were chatting with a man who appeared to have lost something. None of them were looking in her direction.

It's now or never, Sara told herself. She adjusted her glasses, squared her shoulders, and turned the handle. It was unlocked! She cracked the door and slipped inside.

An empty hallway stretched before her. She walked carefully along it. As she approached the end, she heard men's voices.

"Music cue's coming up, but wait for the announcement."

"Okay."

Sara peeked around the corner. What she saw made her eyes widen. The control booth was glassed in. It jutted out over the arena seats, giving a spectacular view of the entire arena.

Sara recognized Charlotte Hartman's father. The big, balding man was sitting at a console, facing a computer screen. His focus was constantly jumping between the screen and the action on the floor. Four men sat beside Mr. Hartman. They were sitting at consoles too. All of the men wore headsets.

Sara recognized only one of the four men—the young blond man. On the night of the spelling bee, he'd been working near the stage.

Mr. Hartman turned toward that man now. "Phil, how's that check on screen seven?"

"It checks okay," he replied.

Sara could see that the men were programming all the special effects in the arena. Over the loudspeakers, there were pre-taped announcements or bursts of rock music. On the giant multimedia screens, there were close-ups of the floor action or still pictures of players with graphics of their statistics.

Sara watched the men work for a few minutes. She listened intensely, hoping Mr. Hartman might talk about his daughter. But he didn't. Mostly what Sara heard was confusing tech speak.

"Sam and Phil, you two can take ten now," Mr. Hartman finally said, checking his watch. "But somebody input the stats on the new players before the start of the second half."

"I'll do it," Phil said.

"Okay, here," Mr. Hartman handed Phil an envelope.

Phil and another man stood up and began to turn around.

Sara tried not to panic. There was no place to hide, so she quickly retraced her steps. She raced back down the corridor, slipped back out the door, and stepped away from it. When the two men exited the control booth, she followed them.

The man named Sam peeled off and headed for a restroom. Phil moved to the escalator, and she stuck with him.

As Phil went down a level, Sara noticed her cousin Keith darting around the Level E refreshment stand. Suddenly, he looked up and saw her on the escalator.

"Sara Bishop!" he called out.

Oh, no, Sara thought.

Phil had heard her name. He glanced wildly around. When he saw Sara standing behind him on the escalator, he said nothing. But Sara was sure he recognized her from the spelling bee.

With a look of panic on his face, Phil stepped off the escalator at Level E. He moved away from Sara as fast as he could.

"Where did you go, Sara?" Keith called, rushing to meet her. "My dad sent me to look for you."

Sara pointed to the blond man in the headset and blue blazer, racing away. "Look," she whispered. "I think that's the man who helped Sara cheat."

"Why him?" Keith asked.

"Mr. Hartman manages the control booth," Sara explained. "I saw it myself. He's way too busy to have gotten near the stage to help his daughter. But that man, Phil, worked on the floor that night. He was close to the stage."

"I remember seeing him, too," Keith admitted.

"He made hand signals all night," Sara noted, "as if he were communicating with someone on stage. He could have been giving clues to Cha-Cha."

Keith nodded. "And he was also wearing a headset."

Sara's brow furrowed. "Why is that important?"

"You can communicate by radio signal with a headset," Keith told her. "You know, like a walkie-talkie?"

"I know, but Charlotte wasn't wearing a head-set. So how was she supposed to hear any clues?"

Keith rolled his eyes. "Haven't you ever seen a spy movie? She could have been wearing a tiny microphone in her ear to receive the signal. Even those wild heart-shaped glasses she was wearing could have held a receiver embedded in the part of the frame that sits near her ear."

"That's true. I hadn't thought of that," Sara said. "But I still think Phil's the key."

"Why?" Keith asked.

"On the night of the bee, while we were waiting near the arena's entrance, I saw Mr. Hartman in the parking lot. He handed Phil an envelope. I didn't think anything of it at the time, but now…"

Keith nodded. "You think Phil was being paid off with some of Cha-Cha's winnings."

"She won five thousand dollars," Sara noted. "I'd say she could afford it."

"Come on. We better get back," Keith said.

As they walked back to their seats, Sara asked her cousin, "What about that anonymous note? Who could have sent it? Do you think it was someone in the control room? Someone who works with Mr. Hartman?"

"It's possible," Keith said. "But almost anything is at this point, including your being wrong."

Mystery #1

Mystery #2

Mystery #3

Sara frowned. "About what?"

"I don't think either Mr. Hartman or anyone who works for him would risk their jobs to help a girl cheat at winning a spelling bee," Keith said. "I still think Dexter Adams is your most likely suspect."

Sara thought that over. "He goes to your school, right?"

"Right," Keith whispered.

Sara smiled. "So when's your next game?"

7. CHA-CHA ENCOUNTER

The Union Junior High gymnasium was packed with kids. Sara sat in the wooden bleachers, watching the basketball players race up and down the court. As usual, her cousin Keith was scoring for his team. When the clock ticked down to halftime, Union was ahead by ten.

Sara wasn't really here to watch the game though. She was here to watch Dexter Adams and Cha-Cha Hartman. At the moment, Dexter was on the gym stage, playing trombone with the school's brass band. Cha-Cha was sitting in the stands, reading a magazine and totally ignoring the court action.

Dexter had ditched his "spelling bee" shirt. Tonight he wore black jeans and a black t-shirt with a big, red broken heart on the front. For some reason, Cha-Cha was dressed the exact same way—black jeans and a black t-shirt with a big red broken heart.

Sara kept a close eye on them both. She was hoping for a chance to ask Cha-Cha an important question—if she could get up the nerve to confront her.

BZZZZZ!

The half-time buzzer rang. The crowd cheered and both teams headed for their locker rooms. Then the cheerleaders ran onto the floor and did their thing. Finally, an adult voice came over the loudspeaker.

"And now, for your entertainment, here's Union Junior High's own slammin' rock band…The Heart Breakers."

Sara was surprised to see that the school's brass band had left the stage. Cha-Cha was now standing up there with Dexter. He'd exchanged his trombone for an electric guitar. Two more boys had joined them—a drummer and a bass guitarist.

Dexter approached the microphone. "Hello, Union! Are you ready to party?"

The crowd cheered and the band began to play. Cha-Cha had a strong singing voice. She sang two numbers in a row. Then the announcer called the cheerleaders back on to do a few more cheers.

Dexter and Cha-Cha left the stage with the other band members. They all headed out a back door exit. Sara figured this was her chance to speak with Cha-Cha, so she climbed down from the bleachers and followed them.

"We are so tight now," the drummer said, rapping his sticks on the concrete wall outside.

The band members were drinking from water bottles and wiping sweat from their brows. The night was cool and the grassy area behind the gym was dimly lit. Sara tried to remain in the shadows, near the propped back door.

"Yeah, we sound pretty good," said the bass guitar player.

"Pretty good?" Dex repeated. "We're awesome! And Cha-Cha's the most awesome of all."

The bass guitarist rolled his eyes. "Well, I hope you're right about our demo."

"I am," Dex said. "Once Cha-Cha appears on national television, we'll rise above the pack. Millions of people are going to hear her sing—"

"Cha-Cha is ready to Cha-Cha!" Charlotte sang out.

In her shadowy hiding place, Sara stifled a groan. *If I hear that stupid line one more time,* she thought, *I'm going to scream!*

"I'm telling you," Dexter continued. "When we send our demo CD to a record company, we'll get a contract like that." He snapped his fingers. "You just wait and see. Cha-Cha on TV will be our edge.

Sara's eyes widened. She could see why Keith thought Dexter might have helped Cha-Cha cheat. She was the lead singer in his band. That meant the more exposure she got, the better it was for The Heart Breakers.

"Who are you?" the drummer suddenly asked. He'd spotted Sara lurking in the shadows.

Sara gulped as the drummer stepped forward and pointed his drumstick in her face. "I'm...uh...n-nobody," she stammered. "Just a fan."

Cha-Cha whipped around. "You!" she cried. "I know you! You're that girl from the spelling bee. Sara Bishop!"

"Nice to see you again," Sara said, edging toward the door. "I'm on my way to get some food now..."

"What are you doing here?" Cha-Cha challenged, striding up to block Sara's escape.

"I'm just here to watch my cousin play basketball," Sara quickly explained.

"Who?" Cha-Cha asked.

"Keith Bishop," Sara said. "He's on your junior high basketball team."

"Oh, Keith... right. I'm in a couple classes with him." Cha-Cha's tense expression relaxed.

"I didn't know you two were related."

Sara was about to dart away when she stopped herself. *Come on, Sara, get brave,* she told herself. *This is your chance.*

Sara swallowed her nerves and cleared her throat. "You know, Charlotte," she began, "I never got to congratulate you. For winning the bee, I mean."

Cha-Cha waved her hand. "That's okay. Things got crazy on stage after I won."

"Your last word was really tough, too," Sara said.

"My last word?" Cha-Cha said. "Yeah...I guess it was."

"By the way," Sara said, "I noticed you didn't ask for a definition before you spelled your word. Why is that?"

"Well, Sara, there's a very good reason I didn't ask for a definition!" Cha-Cha said. She gave a nervous little laugh.

"Well," Sara said, "what is it?"

Cha-Cha threw up her hands. "I knew the word! That's why! I mean, come on, who hasn't heard of Pocahontas? She was a beautiful Indian princess."

"Cha-Cha, let's roll," Dex called, heading back inside the gym.

"Got to go," Cha-Cha said, joining with the rest of Dex's band. "Better luck next year, okay? Bye!"

Sara stood alone in the outside shadows. She felt so many different emotions—shock, anger, disbelief. For the first time since she got that anonymous note, there was no doubt in Sara's mind about whether or not Cha-Cha had cheated.

"Your word wasn't *Pocahontas*," Sara whispered. "It was *pococurante*."

8. NOT SO INSTANT REPLAY

During the next few days, Sara tried to figure out how to prove Cha-Cha cheated. But all she did was fail.

If I can't figure out how Cha-Cha cheated and who helped her, it's over, she thought. *I can't make an accusation without proof. The note isn't enough!*

On Friday morning, she stuffed the anonymous letter into her desk drawer and forgot about it, until Friday night. That's when her cousin Keith came over to baby-sit.

"I brought something with me, Sara," he said after her parents left the house. "I think it's really going to help."

"Help with what?" Sara asked.

Keith stared at her. "Your spelling bee mystery. What else?"

Sara shook her head. "Maybe I should drop the whole thing and just focus on trying to win next year."

"You can't drop it," Keith said.

"I can," Sara shot back. "Charlotte won. If she cheated, she cheated. What can I do about it?"

"You can catch her, that's what. Look, you can't let a

cheater win. If Charlotte cheated, then she cheated everyone, Sara, not just you. And when she goes to the national spelling bee, she might cheat to win that too. Do you really want all those kids who worked as hard as you to be beaten by a fraud?"

"No," she admitted. "When you put it that way, I guess it's worth one more try....What have you got?"

"Beni's video." He pulled the tape out of his backpack. "Remember the night of the regional finals? Benita Wilcox said she'd sell you a copy of her student film. I bought it from her today at school," he said, popping it into the living room player.

The television screen lit up with a familiar sight: the marquee of the Fairfield Sports Arena. Its big colorful letters displayed the date of the regional finals.

While Nina sat coloring on the living room floor, Keith and Sara sat on the couch, closely watching the video. Using the remote, they slowed or stopped the tape so they could really examine what was going on whenever Charlotte walked up to spell a word.

At times, Sara and Keith tried to focus on Cha-Cha's boyfriend. Was he pointing to different letters on his shirt? Or just scratching himself?

They spotted the blond man, Phil, in his navy sports arena blazer and headset. He was speaking into the headset's microphone, but they couldn't tell what he was saying or what his hand signals meant.

"I know the sign language alphabet," Sara said. "And that's not even close."

"They could have worked out a code," Keith suggested.

Finally, after an exhausting two hours, Sara came to her moment of truth. "Ugh," she muttered. "Here it comes again—me messing up the spelling of *antipyretic*."

"I'm thirsty!" Nina announced from the living room floor. She had been eating pretzels, and her juice glass was empty.

Keith got up from the couch. "Come on, Nina," he said. "Bring your glass to the kitchen."

Sara watched herself misspell "antipyretic" again. Then Cha-Cha Hartman waltzed out for her final word, still a stop-sign vision in red hearts from head to toe, including those crazy heart-shaped glasses.

Sara groaned. *I still can't figure out how Cha-Cha cheated*, she thought, *and we're already at the end of the videotape!*

"I guess I have to face reality. She's probably going to get away with cheating," Sara muttered. She slumped forward on the couch, dropping her head in her hands.

"Don't be sad, Sara," Nina said, coming back into the living room. She carried a tall glass of Ruby Juice in her two tiny hands. Hoping to cheer her big sister up, she set the glass down on the coffee table, right in front of Sara. The tall glass blocked Sara's view of the TV, but she didn't bother moving it. She was so down, she just stared at the screen through the glass of translucent red juice.

"Are you ready, Charlotte?" Mr. Fisher asked on the videotape.

"Cha-Cha is ready to Cha-Cha!" Charlotte sang out for the umpteenth time that night.

Just then, the TV screen showed a close-up of one of the sports arena's multimedia screens. As they'd done for the entire bee,

colorful graphics danced all over the screen. Then letters came together and froze in a random, colorful design of illegible text. "Quiet, Please!" appeared over the jumbled letters and a hush fell over the crowd.

An instant later, the sports arena broadcast a huge close-up of Charlotte on the multimedia screen, waving to her boyfriend in the front row. He gave her the elaborate thumbs up. She smiled and adjusted her heart-shaped glasses.

"Stop the tape, Keith!" Sara cried as he walked back into the living room. "Play back the last minute!"

Sara held up the glass of Ruby Juice. Once again, she looked through it, at the TV screen.

"Ohmigosh!" Sara cried. She ran to her room and grabbed her digital camera. Then she took a close-up picture of the TV screen.

"Sara!" Keith cried. "What are you doing? What's going on?"

"I know how Cha-Cha Hartman won the spelling bee!" she cried. "And I'm going to prove it!"

Can you solve the Case of the Suspicious Spelling Bee?

Use the decoder to see the picture that Sara took of the TV screen. This is the same way that Cha-Cha would have seen it. Can you guess who helped Cha-Cha cheat and how? Who do you think sent her the anonymous note? Check the U-Solve-It! web site to see if you're right!

96